The Last Coquí

Story by NANCY ANA PÉREZ

Illustrations by PATRICIA SPEIER-TORRES

LIBROS: Encouraging Cultural Literacy
Long Beach, New York
www.librospress.com

To my three children: Ari, Cristina and Damaris, and the children of Holyoke.   —N.A.P.

To Claus and Mercedes Speier, the best parents anyone could have.   —P.S.T.

LIBROS: Encouraging Cultural Literacy
P.O. Box 453
Long Beach, NY. 11561
Text copyright © 2002 by Nancy Ana Pérez
Illustrations copyright © 2002 by Patricia Speier-Torres.
The text of this book is set in 15 point Arial.
The illustrations are mixed media pastels.
First Edition
Printed in Hong Kong

Publisher's Cataloging-in-Publication
(Provided by Quality Books, Inc.)

Pérez, Nancy Ana.
    The last coqui / story by Nancy Ana Pérez ;
illustrated by Patricia Speier-Torres.
      p. cm.
      Summary: After a hurricane hits his native Puerto
Rico, Coquiki hears he is the last coqui left alive.
Young readers will follow Coquiki and his friends Lady
Hen and Tito the Lizard as they work together in search
of other survivors.
      Audience: Grades 3-8.
      LCCN 2002101682 (English)
      LCCN 2002101683 (Spanish)
      ISBN 0-9675413-4-4 (English)
      ISBN 0-9675413-5-2 (Spanish)

1. Friendship--Juvenile fiction. 2. Cooperation--
Juvenile fiction. 3.Compassion--Juvenile fiction.
[1. Friendship--Fiction. 2. Cooperation--Fiction.
3. Compassion--Fiction.]   I. Speier-Torres, Patricia. II. Title.

PZ7. P42568La2002   [E]
             QBI33-519

One day in Puerto Rico, the island's blue sky disappeared. Dark and angry clouds moved in. Mr. Wind began to blow with mighty strength. And Mrs. Rain started tumbling to the ground. This was no ordinary storm.

It was the hurricane, the most powerful storm of all. The hurricane always tried very hard to destroy anything that got in its way. Very quickly, the animals ran to hide. They knew what to do. This kind of storm wasn't new to them. It came every year.

This hurricane was very mean to the animals. It asked, "Who cares about these animals? If they get in my way, I will blow them away. No one will miss these worthless things."

What a terrible hurricane! You can see what the animals were up against. But all the fierce wind and rain in the world couldn't frighten one of the island's smallest animals, a coquí, like a tiny tree frog. The name of this special coquí was Coquikí.

When the mean hurricane finally went away, it was early in the evening. Very carefully, Coquikí hopped out of his hiding place and started searching for other coquíes. Coquikí sang out into the night air, "ko-kee... ko-kee... ko-kee."

He listened for others, but he heard no reply to his song. Again and again, Coquikí sang his tune, "ko-kee... ko-kee... ko-kee." Again and again, he heard no others. Coquikí was worried and began to think, "Oh my goodness, I can't believe it! It can't be! Am I the last coquí in the world?"

Coquikí sat down to wonder. "What will Puerto Rico be like without our music? Who will sing when the sun goes down? Who will serenade the children to sleep? And the children living in the United States will be sad, too. Who will fill their little hearts with pride and joy?"

As an elder coquí, Coquikí knew what he had to do. He went on a brave journey to search for his coquí friends. Coquikí hopped and hopped, and searched and searched, for days and weeks. His little coquí legs became very tired. But his big coquí heart pushed him on.

One day, Coquikí saw two longtime friends, Lady Hen and Tito the Lizard. Coquikí was so happy to find out that his dear friends had survived the brutal hurricane.

Coquiki quickly asked, "Lady Hen, have you or Tito the Lizard seen any other coquíes?" "No, we haven't," said Lady Hen. Sadly, Coquikí replied, "Oh dear, I was afraid of that."

Lady Hen said, "Dear Coquikí, tell me what's on your mind." Coquikí answered, "I'm feeling very worried. Since the big bad hurricane, I haven't seen or heard any other coquies. I've been hopping and hopping, and searching and searching, for weeks. I just can't find my friends."

Coquikí paused for a moment. Then, said, "My dear friends, I don't want to complain. It's just that all this hopping and hopping hasn't been easy for me. I don't know how much farther my little coquí body can go. My coquí legs are tired and sore."

Lady Hen and Tito the Lizard listened as Coquikí continued his story. "I have no time to rest. I search all day, and I search all night. I hop all day, and I sing all night. I feel tired all day, and I feel lonely all night." Coquikí paused again and said, "You just can't imagine how alone I feel at night. Gone are the glorious melodies of my coquí clan.

Each and every night, I sing out to my coquí brothers and sisters. I always use my most precious coquí voice. I sing out, 'ko-kee... ko-kee... ko-kee.' No coquí returns my song. I sing out again and again, 'ko-kee... ko-kee... ko-keeeeeeeee...' In return, I hear only a sickly silence. Maybe I am the last coquí!"

Coquikí's sad eyes were filled with tears. He asked his two friends, "What should I do?" Lady Hen didn't say a word. Instead, she sat down on a nearby rock to think. In the meantime, Tito the Lizard tried to comfort his distressed coquí friend.

"My brother," he said, "the evil hurricane has robbed us all by silencing our nights. How we all miss the soothing coquí song! But we will not despair. Brother coquí, no storm is strong enough to defeat us. Let us work together to find your brothers and sisters. I will carry you on my back, so you can rest your tired coquí legs." Coquikí happily hopped onto Tito the Lizard's back.

Right away, Tito the Lizard took Coquikí to the rock where Lady Hen was sitting. Coquikí bowed his head before the grand lady and asked her, "Lady Hen, will you join us in our search for other coquíes? Please say 'yes.' We desperately need your help. No one else can do the things you do."

All the animals knew about Lady Hen's very special talent. It was no secret that she could foresee the future. She was always being sought out by the animals. They came to her to find out what would happen to them tomorrow or the next day. Coquikí was certain that if there were other coquíes, the wise hen would know how, when, and where they would be found.

Lady Hen continued to sit quietly on the rock. With eyes closed, she was in deep thought. All of a sudden, Lady Hen's eyes opened wide, and the wise lady spoke.

"My dear Coquikí, listen to me. My thoughts tell me that you won't find your friends without me. So, as your friend, it's my duty to help you. Together we can save the glorious melodies of your coquí clan." Lady Hen stood up and walked towards a narrow path. "We must go this way," she said.

The three friends walked on that narrow path for many hours. Coquikí was feeling very eager to see the face of another coquí. Then, all of a sudden, his teeny tiny coquí heart began to beat faster. "Oh my," he thought to himself, "our search is almost over. I feel it." Soon thereafter, the three animal friends came to a crossing in the path. Lady Hen shouted, "Halt!"

Then she said, "We will wait here. My thoughts tell me that in a short while, a boy leading a burro by a rope will appear. This boy is very tired. You will see his young forehead dripping with sweat. This boy's burro is tired as well. You will see his burro's back carrying a large load of bananas and mangoes. We must wait for the boy and burro to appear." Coquikí and Tito the Lizard didn't know what to expect next.

In an instant, Tito the Lizard and Coquikí spotted the boy and his burro. The boy was heading straight towards the three friends. He came closer and closer to them. Then, he crossed in front of Coquikí. He was so close, Coquikí could've reached out and touched him. The boy was walking very slowly. He looked so tired. Indeed, there was much sweat on his young forehead.

The burro looked tired as well. His load was heavy. And, there were many bananas and mangoes on his burro's back. Amazing! Lady Hen had predicted the future perfectly. Tito the Lizard and Coquikí were completely dazzled by the amazing Lady Hen. They simply couldn't wait to see what would happen next.

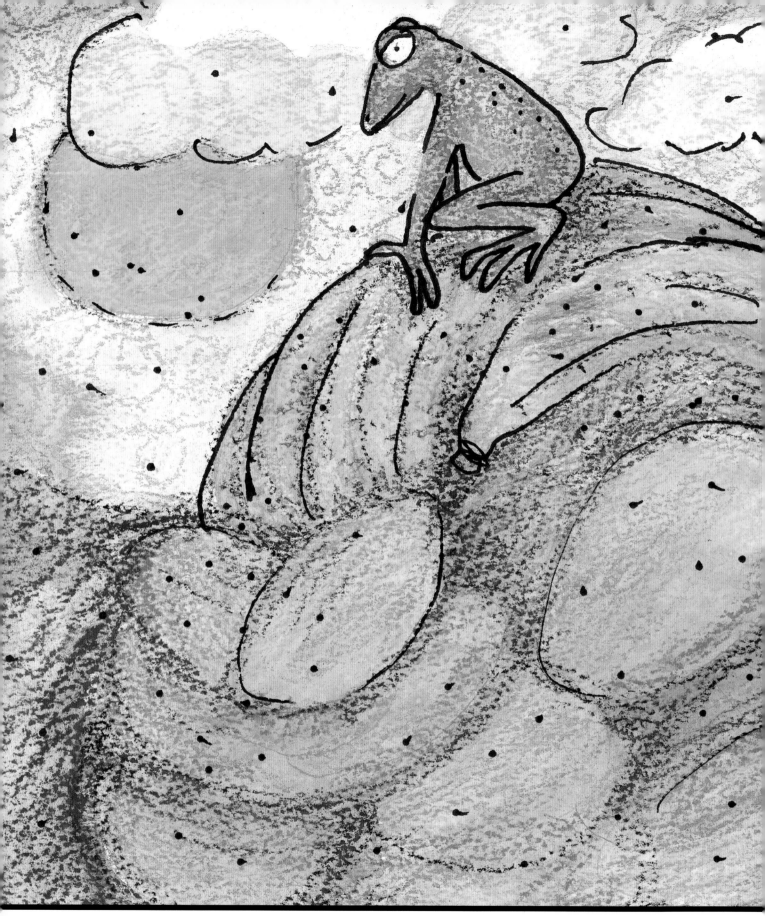

By this time, the sun was beginning to set across the island. Coquikí's heart was beating faster and faster especially as the burro passed in front of him. Coquikí knew there must be something special about that burro. He looked at him very carefully. Then he saw something wonderful! The burro had a most precious passenger. With joy, Coquikí hopped down from Tito the Lizard's back.

Immediately, he sang out, "ko-kee... ko-kee... ko-kee." At once, the burro's passenger heard his song. She sat up straight and looked down towards Coquikí. Then with a big hop of joy, she leaped from the burro's back and landed right in front of Coquikí. "My name is Coquiana," she said. "For weeks and months, I have been hopping and hopping, and searching and searching, for other coquíes. Finally, my search has ended."

"I am Coquikí! For weeks and months, I worried that I was the last coquí. And now today, thanks to the help of my very dear friends, Tito the Lizard and Lady Hen, I worry no more." Then he shouted out into the Caribbean evening, "I am not the last coquí!" He began to sing joyously, "ko-kee... ko-kee... ko-kee" while Coquiana danced by his side. Lady Hen walked over to the new coquí couple.

Proudly, she gave them her blessing and said to them, "Dear ones, my thoughts tell me of our future. The nighttime on our island will return to its glorious splendor. You will fill the warm air with the ko-kee melodies of your clan. Your children and your children's children will make this so. Go now, Coquikí and Coquiana! Go out into the night and make us all proud."

. . .and that's exactly what they did.